Albie
and the
Space Rocket

FOR MY DAD, WHO KNEW ALBIE WELL,
AND FOR GUY AND DAVID

First published in hardback in Great Britain by HarperCollins Publishers Ltd in 2003
First published in paperback by Collins Picture Books in 2003

This edition published in 2010

1 3 5 7 9 10 8 6 4 2
ISBN 13: 978-0-00-786522-2

Collins Picture Books is an imprint of the Children's Division, part of HarperCollins Publishers Ltd.

Text copyright © Andy Cutbill/Ripping Gags Ltd 2003
Illustrations copyright Andy Cutbill/Ripping Gags Ltd and HarperCollins Publishers Ltd 2003

Based on the television series *Albie* © Cosgrove Hall Films Ltd

The author and illustrators assert the moral right to be identified
as the author and illustrators of the work.
A CIP catalogue record for this title is available from the British Library.

The HarperCollins website address is: www.harpercollins.co.uk

Printed and bound in Thailand

Albie
and the
(super-duper, intergalactic)
Space Rocket

by Andy Cutbill

ILLUSTRATIONS BY

Andy Cutbill and Mark Stacey

HarperCollins *Children's Books*

It was just another ordinary night.

Albie was sleeping peacefully when…

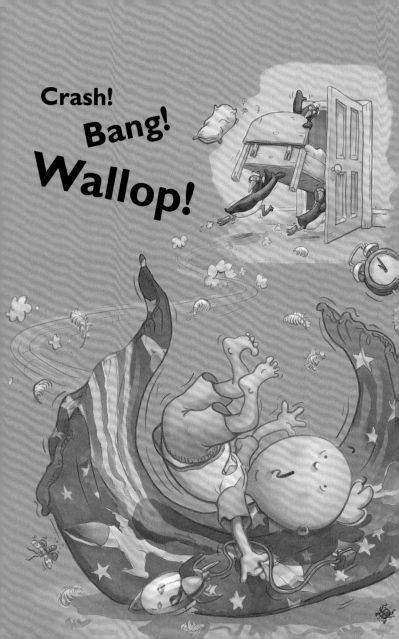

"**Flips!**" shrieked Albie. "Come back here with my bed!"

He grabbed his torch and raced out of the room.

At the bottom of the stairs Albie heard noises. Bravely, he peered round a door and found...

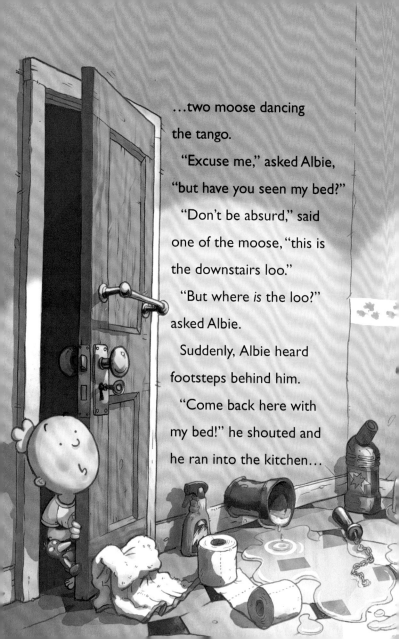

...two moose dancing the tango.

"Excuse me," asked Albie, "but have you seen my bed?"

"Don't be absurd," said one of the moose, "this is the downstairs loo."

"But where *is* the loo?" asked Albie.

Suddenly, Albie heard footsteps behind him.

"Come back here with my bed!" he shouted and he ran into the kitchen...

"Ahhhh!" yelled Albie as he slipped on the
kitchen floor. "Baked beans?"

"Shhh!" whispered a zebra.

"Why?" said Albie. "Is the bed-pincher nearby?"

"Nah," said the zebra…

Albie searched the whole house for his bed.

In the cupboard
under the stairs.

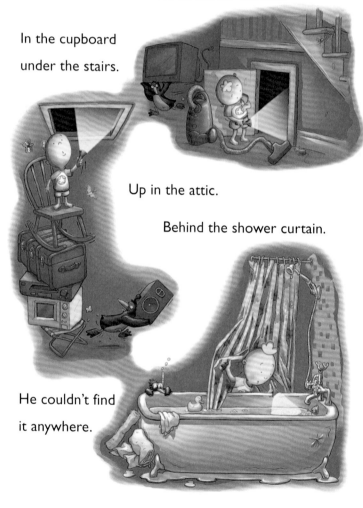

Up in the attic.

Behind the shower curtain.

He couldn't find
it anywhere.

But there was still one room he hadn't checked.

Taking a deep breath, Albie opened the door
and found…

…a herd of quivering ELEPHANTS.

"AHHH!" screamed the elephants.

"Sorry to bother you," said Albie,
"but have you seen my bed?"

"No!" said one of the
elephants.

"So what's that over there?"
asked Albie.

"That?" said another elephant.
"Oh, that's just…"

"...a super-duper, intergalactic space rocket."

"But it's built from my bed!" spluttered Albie.

"And the cooker *and* the downstairs loo!"

"It's state-of-the-art," said the elephant.

"People will go mad when they see this."

"My mum'll go *bonkers*," said Albie.

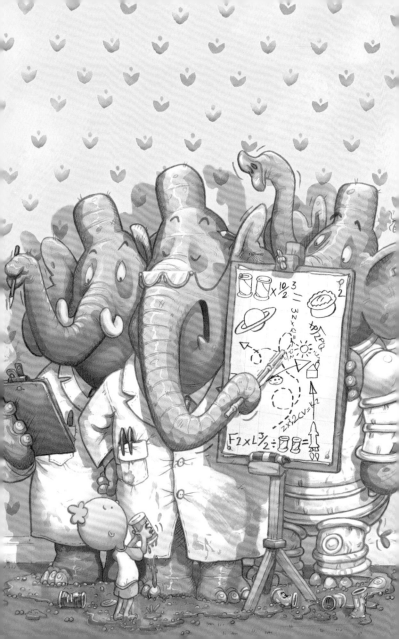

"Well, you can't have it back," said an elephant, "it's almost time for blast off."

"Is my bed going somewhere?" asked Albie.

"To the planet Jupiter, of course!" said the elephants, proudly. "Powered by baked beans."

"But how am I going to sleep without my bed?" asked Albie.

"Don't ask us," said the elephants. "Ask the blokes behind you – *they* nicked it."

Albie spun round to find...

…an entire colony of PENGUINS!

"Got the space helmet!" cried a penguin.

"But you can't have that," shrieked Albie.
"That's my sister Mary's goldfish bowl!"

"It's OK. She won't notice a
thing!" said the penguin.

"**ALLBBB**iiii!!!!!!!eeeeeee
eeeeee!" screeched
Mary from upstairs.
"Where's my goldfish bowl?"
"Don't panic," said
an elephant…

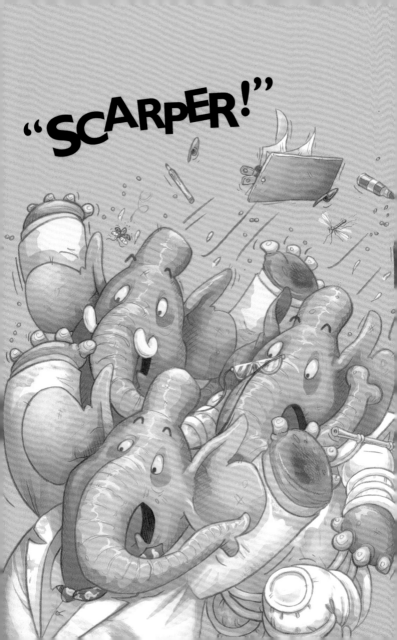

Albie jumped on to the rocket.

"You're not going *anywhere* with my bed!"
he cried.

"Five seconds until blast off!" shouted
the penguin.

"What?" panicked Albie. "Who's driving?"

"You are!" said the penguin,
and he stuck the goldfish
bowl on Albie's head.

"Five!"

Albie fastened

his seat belt...

"Four!"

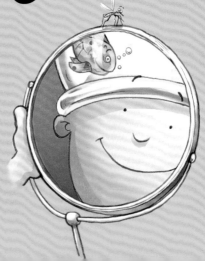

...adjusted the

wing mirrors...

"Three!"

...took off the
handbrake...

"Two!"

...and braced himself
for take off.

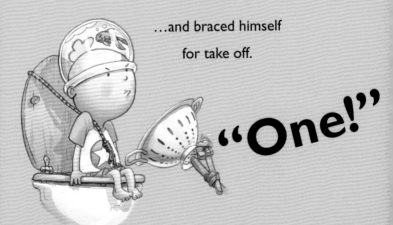

"One!"

"BLAST
IT, ALBIE!"

screamed Mary.

"What's my goldfish bowl doing

on your head?"

"It's the penguins' space helmet," said Albie, jumping off the rocket.

"PENGUINS?" yelled Mary. "Have you gone bonkers? I'm going to wake up Mum."

"B-but…" stuttered Albie. "The elephants built a space rocket with fuel made from baked beans!"

"Albie, not even *elephants* can make rocket fuel from baked beans," said Mary, reaching for the launch button to prove it.

"DON'T PUSH THAT!" yelled Albie…

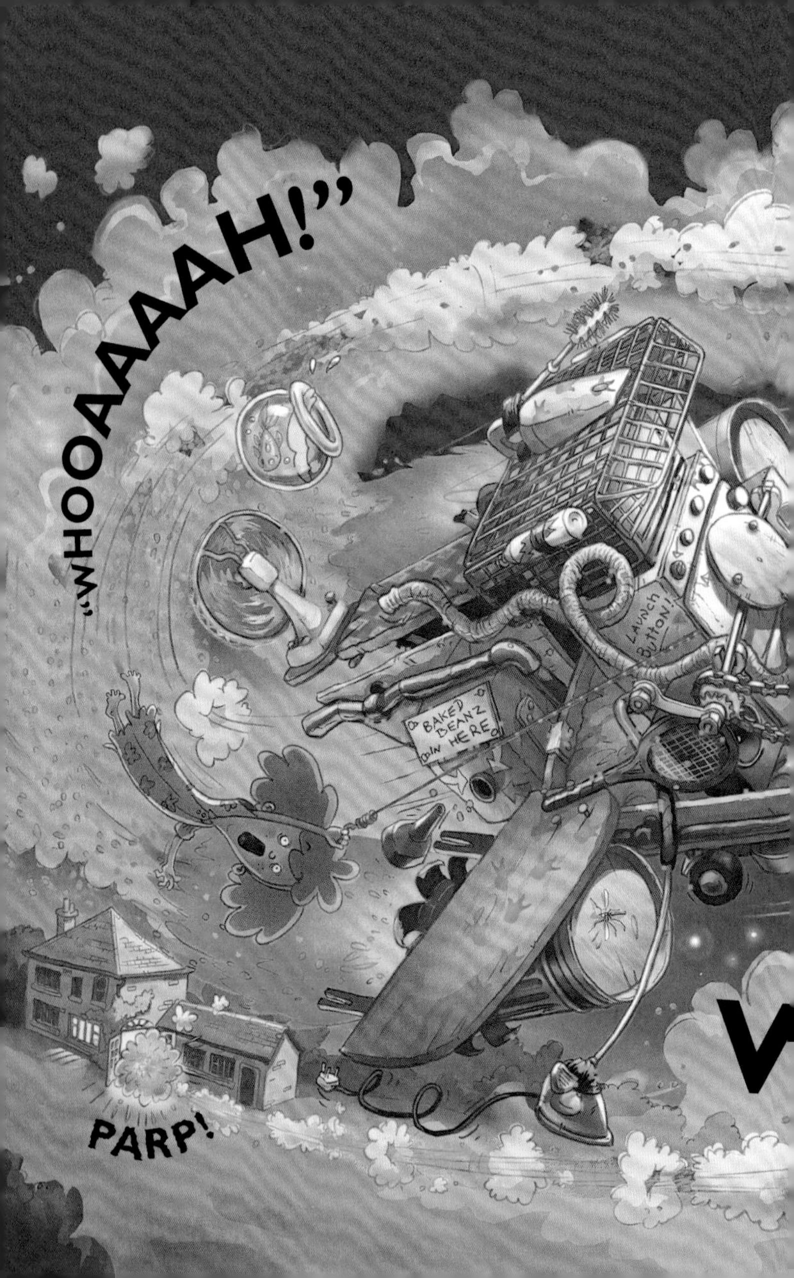
"WHOOAAAAAH!"
LAUNCH BUTTON!
BAKED BEANZ IN HERE
PARP!
W

"**ALBIEEEEEEEEEE!**"

"Oh, flips," said Albie.